SMART in pink!

SMART pink!
in

What Do You Think?

patricia maynard

iUniverse®

SMART IN PINK!
WHAT DO YOU THINK?

iUniverse books may be ordered through booksellers or by contacting:

iUniverse
1663 Liberty Drive
Bloomington, IN 47403
www.iuniverse.com
1-800-Authors (1-800-288-4677)

ISBN: 978-1-4917-5574-7 (sc)
ISBN: 978-1-4917-5576-1 (hc)
ISBN: 978-1-4917-5575-4 (e)

Library of Congress Control Number: 2014921952

Print information available on the last page.

iUniverse rev. date: 04/22/2015

To my best friend, Judith Smith; my cousin, Veronica Benders; and the Progressive and Ambitious Girls Club, who have helped to inspire me in my writings.

I founded the Girls Club to establish a mentorship program for girls in grades three through six. The girls are involved in activities that help them to build their self-esteem and grow spiritually, academically, and socially.

Contents

Part 1

Mom and Dad Sharing and Bonding Time

Mom said the house was decorated with pink ribbons and streamers the day she brought me home from the hospital. She also said there was a big sign on the door that read "Welcome Home! It's a Girl!" The sign was done in bright-pink letters.

I smiled as she recalled my homecoming. "Mom, can you tell me more about me?"

She said, "Yes, dear, I will tell you. The day we left the hospital, I dressed you up in the pretty pink outfit I bought for you. It had matching booties and

1

a cute little pink ribbon for your hair. After I got you dressed, I picked you up in my arms and kissed you. You looked so beautiful, and those bright eyes of yours looked up at me. I was so happy to have my most precious possession in my arms. You snuggled up to me and settled yourself in as if you belonged right where you were. I looked up to heaven and said, 'Thank you, Lord, for hearing and answering my prayer.' When I was pregnant with you, I prayed to the Lord many times for a girl. I would look up and say, 'Lord, please bless me with a girl.' And he did answer my prayer. You were always special to me from the day you were born."

I felt so happy and proud to hear my mom recall this. I knew my mom loved me unconditionally. Whenever I said, "Mom, may I …?" she would say, "Yes, dear!" I love my mom dearly. She made sure I had everything I needed. She bought me the prettiest and cutest dresses and shoes. I felt pampered and spoiled.

On the other hand, my dad was very firm and sometimes stern. I can still hear his deep, husky voice say, "Sara, you need to eat your vegetables! Take your foot off the furniture! Don't go outside without your shoes! Sit up in your chair! Do not slouch! Did you do your homework?" It seems as if he always caught me doing something wrong. When he was in a good mood, he would call out, "Pinky, what did you learn today?" He said that I earned that name because pink was my favorite color, and I always wanted everything in that color. I love when my dad called me Pinky; that was my invitation to talk to him about anything. It was also my time to snuggle up close to him on the couch and talk my heart out. I'd enjoy spending time with him and talking to him about all the things I did that day.

"Dad, my teacher called on me to spell the word of the day and give the meaning. I jumped out of my seat, and in a nice, loud voice I spelled the word and gave the meaning correctly. My teacher said, 'Sara, you are so smart, and that response was correct. Here is your sticker.' I was so happy to receive my sticker. It said 'Good Speller!' I wore it on my chest proudly for the rest of the day. Teachers and students congratulated me, but there were other students who were mad at me and called me names like nerd, brainiac, and bookworm. I just laughed. My friend Monica said she wondered why I don't get mad when they call me those names. I told her I don't mind—I like to be called those names. I felt important and special. She said she didn't understand that because if anyone did that to her, she would make them eat their words. I tried to explain to her that there was no need to do that and that she should make other choices, like ignoring them. If she felt bullied, she should report it. She listened to me and then replied, 'Nobody is going to get away calling me names!' The bell rang, and we had to go back to class, but I planned to continue this conversation. I have to convince Monica that fighting doesn't solve problems—it only helps to create more problems."

Dad said, "You are right, Pinky. Violence only begets violence."

I replied, "Beget? Is that a new word? I will write it down and look up the meaning. I am going to be the next spelling bee champion. I have to learn lots of new words and their meanings." I ran to my room and got my dictionary and thesaurus. I searched for the word, and when I found it, I shouted, "Dad, I just learned a new word and its meaning!"

Then I thought this was a good time to remind him about the computer or iPad he promised to buy for me after he saw my next report card. I said, "Dad, please remember to keep your promise!"

He replied, "Which one?"

I quickly reminded him how much I needed the technology. I pointed out to him how important it was for me to have a computer or an iPad. I said, "Dad, technology is my gateway to the world. There is so much to learn, and this will help me do it. I want to broaden my horizons. I want to learn lots of new words. My vocabulary and my knowledge will increase. You promised to reward me for doing well in school and for my good behavior. Now is the time. I am well behaved, I have excellent grades, and I am the smartest in my class. My teacher said this is the age of technology. That is another new word I learnt, and it is also one of my spelling bee words. She also said this is the twenty-first century, and we all have to be ready to take on the world. We must prepare ourselves and learn as much as we can. I want to do that. I could do so much more if I had my own computer. I would learn new words and explore their meanings. I can also do research for my other classes."

Dad looked at me and said, "Okay, Pinky. You will have your computer next week when I get my paycheck. I won't wait till report card time. I believe in you and I know you will do well. You got most of your smart genes from me, and the rest came from your mom."

I said, "Really, Dad?"

He had this big grin on his face. Then he said, "How about the math? How are you doing with that?"

I replied, "Oh, Dad, don't worry about that. I am good at math, too. I like the word problems; they make me think hard and figure things out. My teacher said once we can analyze things and find a solution that is called critical thinking. You know, Dad, I think school is cool, and I follow the rules." Then I stood up, put my hands on my hips, and looked him in the eyes. "Dad, your daughter is not a fool. I learn well in school"

He reached out his hand, patted me on the head, and said, "That's my girl! You can and you will be anything you want to be. Dream big!"

I liked when my dad talked to me like that. It made me feel powerful. I really wanted to make my mom and dad proud of me.

After I finished talking to him, I ran into the kitchen to find my mom. She was busy cooking dinner. I smelled the food as I walked into the kitchen. She was cooking one of my favorite dishes: mashed potatoes, stewed chicken, and corn on the cob. I was really feeling hungry, and my stomach started growling. I smacked my lips as I thought about my dinner. I skipped lunch today at school because I'd gone to Spelling Bee practice. I didn't want to miss anything. I had already decided I was going to be the Spelling Bee Champion, and I was determined to work hard for it.

"Hi, Mom! I was just talking with Dad."

Mom replied, "What were you two talking about?"

I responded, "It was about my day at school. Mom, I like when he asks me about school. This gave me a chance to tell him all the fun things I did. I also told him about the things that bother me. Mom, did you know he takes the time to listen to me and ask me questions? I like chatting with my dad. He can be the best dad when he wants to be."

Mom and I laughed. Then Mom asked, "What was it you wanted, dear?"

I said, "My teacher picked me to be in the Spelling Bee Competition. She said I was a very good speller. I have to go every day after lunch to practice. The Spelling Bee is in two weeks, and I can't wait to hear them announce, 'The Spelling Bee Champion is Sara Primus!' Mom, you and Dad have to be there to give the loudest applause and cheer."

My mom laughed again and then started to clap. "Yes, yes! We will be there. Now come, Sara. I will put dinner on the table so that you can eat, and then you can do your homework. Go wash your hands, and then tell your dad dinner is on the table."

I replied, "But wait, Mom. Can we talk about what I am going to wear to the Spelling Bee?"

"Sara, one thing is for sure: I know what the color is. For you, it has to be pink! You know, the other day I looked in your clothes closet, and all I saw was pink. You have pink socks, pink panties, pink pants, pink blouses, and oh too many pink dresses. Sara, don't you think it is time to change your color?"

I stood there silently thinking, *not now! I have to go shopping to pick out what might be my last pink outfit.* Mom had been trying real hard to get me to make the change, ever since I was in fourth grade. She said I should choose other colors.

Here I am now taking a trip down memory lane. I recalled the day my mom told me about my kindergarten promotion. I felt so happy and proud to hear my mom talk about the event. She said I looked like a princess. She also said I was wearing a pink ballerina dress, pink socks, and pink ribbons in my hair. I ran up excitedly to receive my awards and prizes. My mom said the audience cheered loudly when my kindergarten teacher announced I was at the top of my class, and then she explained to them how smart and curious I was. She said the teacher told her I was always asking questions. Yep, that was me! My first grade teacher, my second grade teacher, and even my third grade teacher would say to me, "Sara, you ask too many questions," or, "Sara, give someone else a chance to answer," or "Sara you finished too quickly." I was eager to learn. I loved school.

I smiled to myself as I recalled a Valentine's Day fashion show. The other contestants were fussing about whether they should wear red or red and white. My mind was already made up about what I was going to wear: pink was my color. I was wearing a pink pant suit, a pink beaded necklace with various shades of pink, and pink sandals. To top it off, I wore a matching pink hat with bright pink flowers. As I walked across the stage, my heart was beating wildly in my chest, but as I strutted across the stage, I felt good because I knew I looked beautiful. I felt beautiful on the inside and on the outside.

I loved to dress up. One day my auntie Brenda said to me, "Child, you are too full of yourself. You love too much glamour and style. I guess you will grow up to be a fashionista."

I said, "A what? I have to write that word down and look it up in the dictionary."

My aunt laughed and then said, "There you go again, Miss Researcher. I don't think you will find that one there. It is one of those colloquial expressions to describe a person who loves fashion and loves to dress up. You can find the word colloquial in the dictionary; you can look that one up."

I responded, "Okay, I will if you tell me how to spell it." I went to my room, got my school bag, and took out my spelling copy book. She took the pencil and paper from me, spelled it out, and wrote it. I thanked her for teaching me another new word. I also told her I got picked to be in the Spelling Bee, and I showed her my sticker.

She congratulated me, and then she said, "You go, girl!"

In the midst of my daydreaming, I heard my mom saying, "Sara, go wash your hands, and then call Dad for dinner." I jumped up quickly from the chair and ran off the bathroom.

Part 2

Preparation and winning the Spelling Bee

The next two weeks were very busy and exciting for me as I prepared for the Spelling Bee and looked forward to my dad purchasing my new computer. We drilled and practiced that spelling list. The coordinator, Mrs. Phillips, sometimes asked me to help out when she stepped out to make copies of the rules or to do other things. I enjoyed working with my peers because they helped me as much as I helped them. There were fifteen participants, five boys and ten girls. We practiced daily for the competition, and

Mrs. Phillip made sure she prepared us well. We also took on responsibility for ourselves. Every spare time we had, we used it to practice our spelling list. We spent so much time together that we became close friends.

One day I came up with an idea, and I decided to share it with the other spellers. I knew it wouldn't be hard convincing the girls, but I wondered about the boys. I decided I would share it, so I said, "Hey, spellers! What do you think if we all wore pink T-shirts for the competition that said, 'I wear Pink. I always think'?"

Two of the boys, Trevor, Seymour, and all of the girls agreed, but the other three boys said, "Pink is for girls! Why do we have to wear pink? Why can't we wear blue?"

I had to think fast and try to talk them into wearing the pink T-shirts. "The message we want to get out to the others is: no matter what, think! Do you get it? Let us show them it does not matter what color we wear, we are always thinking."

The boys listened, and then they huddled together and whispered back and forth to each other. I waited patiently for their decision. Then Trevor spoke for the group. "We agree. We will do it this time."

We told Mrs. Phillips what we wanted to do, and she liked the idea. She said she thought it was cute and the message was good. She ordered our t-shirts. I organized a group of our classmates to be our cheering squad. I gave them posters with just one word written big and bold on it: "Smart in Pink! Think!" This was to help motivate us.

On the day of the Spelling Bee, everyone was excited. Our parents came out to support us. At nine o'clock we all went to the auditorium. We picked our numbers, hung them around our necks, and sat in our places. The principal, Mrs. Kelly, welcomed everyone. Then Mrs. Phillips, the coordinator, read the rules and introduced the pronouncers, time keeper, and judges.

Soon the focus was on us, and we had to introduce ourselves. The boys seemed shy and even more nervous than the girls. I looked over at my friend Monica and gave her thumbs-up; she waved to me. I felt a little bit nervous, but I had one thing in mind: I would be the Spelling Bee Champion.

The practice round went off smoothly. In the first round, two boys went out. The second round went a little longer. In these early rounds, the words seemed so easy. The third and fourth round the words got a little more challenging: four girls misspelled their word and they went out of the competition, which left nine of us, three boys and six girls. I looked out in the audience and saw my mom and dad; I smiled at them, and they waved to me.

In the sixth round two more boys and one girl misspelled their words and were out of the competition. I started to get anxious and tapped my feet softly on the floor. I had to stay focus and keep my thinking cap on. Every time it was my turn to spell a word, I would use all my options. I would say, "Can I have a sentence please? Can I have the definition? Give me the next pronouncer, please! What is the origin of the word?" I used all these tips to formulate the word in my mind, and then I would carefully and correctly spell the word. It sounded so good to hear the judge say, "Correct!' I clapped my hands and said, "Yes, I've got this!"

In the eighth round three girls misspelled their words. One of them ran off the stage crying, and her mother had to help comfort her. She was crying uncontrollably.

After this, the real competition began with my best friend Monica, three other girls, the last boy, and me. We were all good spellers who were very competitive. We moved to the front row, and most of us sat on the edge of our seats.

The pronouncer said, "Moving right along—round number nine is coming up! Spellers, are you ready?"

We shouted out, "Yes, we are ready!"

Then she said, "The word is perennial."

It was Monica's turn to spell, and she stepped up to the microphone and spelled out the word. She said, "P-e-r-e-n-n-i-a-l."

Then our cheering squad stood up, pushed up their posters, and chanted, "Think! Think! Think!

In the tenth round three of the girls misspelled their words, and that meant they were out of the competition. The excitement continued to build up. My heart and my thoughts were racing. I kept telling myself, *you are the winner.* There were three of us left in the competition: Monica, my best friend; Tony, who was the only boy; and I.

The pronouncer said, "We are now starting round eleventh round. The word is metamorphosis!" Monica stepped up to the microphone and started spelling the word. She said, "M-e-t-a- m-o-r-f-o-s-i-s." She misspelled the word, and the bell rang indicating that the word was spelled wrong. Monica shouted, "Oh no! I messed up!" I walked over to her and gave her a hug, and then she walked slowly off the stage. As I watched her walk off the stage, I felt very sad, however I told myself I had to keep calm and stay focused.

In the twelfth round I sat up in my seat very alert, my eyes fixed on the pronouncer. She said, "This is the twelfth round, and the word is euphemism!"

It was Tony's turn to spell the word. I bowed my head, sounded out the word in my head, broke it down into syllables, thought of the origin, and then thought, *I've got this.* I started smiling and gazed up at him. He was very hesitant to spell the word; he shifted his feet rocked from side to side, and then he attempted to spell the word. He said, "E-u-f-a ..." He stopped and started, pounding his right fist into his left hand. After a few minutes he walked back to his seat, muttering under his breath.

I jumped up from my seat even before the announcer said, "Next speller." Then I remembered the rule and waited until she said, "If this speller spells this word correctly, and then the next word, she will be the winner." Then she repeated the word: euphemism.

I walked briskly to the microphone and said, "Next pronouncer, please! The next pronouncer repeated the word. Then I said, 'Sentence, please!' The pronouncer read a sentence using the word. My next response was, 'Definition, please!' I continued my questioning, 'What is the language of origin?" After I received the answers, I said, "Thank you!"

Just before I spelled the word, I looked out in the audience for my mom and dad. As my eyes met theirs, my dad stood up and said, "You can do it, Pinky! We believe in you!" Then my mom popped up beside my dad and shouted, "You've got this! Go for it!"

I gave them a big grin, and then I spoke loudly into the microphone. "I will now spell the word. E-U-P-H-E-M-I-S-M."

The judge responded, "Correct!"

Then the pronouncer said, "The next word is carcinogenic."

I took a deep breath and then continued with my routine questions.

"Can you repeat the word?

Can I have the next pronouncer?

Can I have the definition?

Can I have the word in a sentence?"

After I clearly, carefully, calmly, and confidently asked my tip questions, I said, "I am now ready to spell my word: C-A-R-C-I-N-O- G-E-N-I-C."

I heard the judge say, "Correct!" Then the pronouncer said, "We have our Spelling Bee Champion!"

The audience gave a thunderous applause.

My cheering squad shouted, "Smart in pink! What do you think?"

All the boys in their pink T-shirts ran up and hugged me. It really felt good to be hugged by all those boys.

Then I felt my feet lifted from the floor. My dad ran on to the stage, picked me up, and hoisted me to his shoulders to spin me around. I was elated, and my head felt giddy. I hugged my dad's head tightly because I didn't want to fall down. Wow, I did it—I was the Spelling Bee Champion!

After things settled down, the Spelling Bee coordinator, Mrs. Phillips, presented me with a "Top Speller" medal, a certificate, and a trophy. I also received a gift bag with goodies. I couldn't wait to look inside. However, I had to pose for many pictures so I'll do that later. I felt great and gave them my best smile as I held my big trophy high. The first and second runners-up also received prizes, and we took a group picture together. Tony was the only boy that was left in the competition, and so Monica and I sandwiched him. We placed him in the middle, and as we posed for the pictures, we snuggled up to him and gave the biggest smiles.

As I rode back home with Mom and Dad in the car, my mom told me how proud I made her feel. Then my dad said, "My daughter showed me today what she is capable of. I believed in her and knew she could do it, but she also showed me she could. Pinky you've got what it takes. Keep doing your best!"

I felt like I was floating on cloud nine, to hear my dad saying all these wonderful things about me.

Dad pulled the car into the driveway, and as we walked to the door, he said, "There is a surprise inside for you."

I responded, "Hurry, Mom, open the door!" She quickly turned the key in the lock and opened the door. I pushed past her and looked around. There on the table was a box wrapped with beautiful pink paper and pink ribbons wrapped around it. I rushed over, picked it up, and instantly knew what it was. It was my computer! I ran to my dad and hugged him. "Thank you, Daddy!" Then I hugged my mom and kissed her. I also said, "Both of you are the best parents in the world." They laughed.

I ripped off the ribbon and paper and shouted, "I got what I wanted!"

The next morning as I was getting ready for school, I was in the bathroom brushing my teeth. I heard my mom calling my name. "Sara! Sara, come and see this!" I finished brushing my teeth and washing my face, and then I ran into the kitchen to find my mom. She held up the newspaper and said, "Look at this! You are a star."

I read the headlines written in big bold letters.
Spelling Bee Champion!
She Is Smart in Pink, and She Can Think!

I read it and smiled, and then I turned to Mom and said, "He left out a few words.

She turned to me and said, "What words were left out?"

"It should have said, 'She is pretty and smart in pink and she can think.' I think I will call Damien, the reporter, and tell him thanks, but I will also tell him about the few words he left out. I don't think he will get mad at me—in fact I think he will agree with me. He knows I buy the paper and read his articles."

Mom laughed and said, "That is a good idea. Sara, I like the way you think and feel about yourself. I think and feel the same way, too. You show a lot of self-confidence. You've got what it takes to get the job done."

I could do anything I set my mind to do. If I believed it, then I could achieve it.

I loved school. Every morning I got out of bed and was excited about going to school. Thoughts were flowing in my head about things I wanted to do that day. My grades were good, I had many friends, and my teacher praised and encouraged me every day. I maintained good study habits, stayed positive, and set goals for my future.

My friends and I arrived early to school every day because we loved to play and have fun. Before school started, we would skip and jump rope, played with the hula hoops, played tag, and other ring games. We even raced each other to the bathroom or the water fountain. We had lots of fun. Even the boys would join with us and have fun. However, other times the boys would be mean to us and take away our ropes.

They took our ropes and tried to engage us in games of tug-of-war. Several times they managed to pull us down. One day we surprised them and pulled them all down. This made them stay away from us for a while! We always planned and prepared for them. We had some competitions with them in the races featuring boys against girls. They won some, and we won some. School days were happy days.

Part 3

Bullying events after the Spelling Bee Competition

There were still a few students who tried to bully me with name calling and a few wicked pranks. One of my worst days with the bullies was on that Monday after the Spelling Bee. It seemed as if they planned for me that weekend.

As I walked through the school gate extra early that Monday morning, I saw the group that always seemed to be up to no good. They huddled closer together as I walked past them. Then all of a sudden I felt a sharp pain. Something hit in my back, and

I heard someone say, "This is for the champion!" I turned around quickly and angrily, and I saw the boys in the group running away. I looked around to see what they threw at me; it was a rock.

I picked it up and took it to the principal's office. I explained to her what happened, and I identified the boys I saw in the group: Keith, Willy, Larry, and Dennis. Mrs. Kelly was a good principal; she was fair and looked out for all the children. She got upset when I told her what happened. She apologized to me for what happened, and then she sent me to Mrs. Cornelius, the nurse, to check my back.

The nurse looked at my back and said there was a slight bruise. She cleaned it with some peroxide, and she sent me back to the principal. Mrs. Kelly sent for the boys. They tried to put the blame on Keith because he was the biggest one in the group. I knew he didn't do it—he was not a leader, he was a follower. I had an idea who threw the rock because he was the most aggressive and disruptive one in the bunch, and his teacher complained about him all the time. He always called me names. Finally, Mrs. Kelly got them to admit it was Dennis, who was in the other sixth grade class. She sent for him and gave him a letter to inform his parents that they had to attend a mandatory parent meeting. She also instructed the secretary to call his parents and let them know what he did.

Mrs. Kelly then called my mom, told her what happened, and informed her about the meeting. Then she called the counselor, Mrs. Newton, and instructed her to get the fifth and sixth grade classes together to address the issue of bullying and its consequences.

All the classes assembled in the auditorium. The counselor greeted us warmly, and then she said, "Today we are going to discuss the topic of bullying. Has anyone of you in here ever been bullied? Indicate this by raising your hands." Several hands went up. The counselor responded, "Oh no! This is not a good thing, and this should not happen to any of you. Bullying is hurtful and dangerous, and it is also a crime. Anyone who has been bullied must report it. Don't stay silent and allow it to continue. You must speak up!"

She paused and then said, "Bullies put others down to make themselves feel more powerful. Bullies like to dominate others. Bullies try to manipulate others sometimes in a smart and deceptive way." Everyone was sitting quietly and listening intently. They suddenly came alive when the counselor shouted, "We don't want any bullying here at this school! Students, stand and repeat this."

We stood up and in our loudest voices shouted, "We don't want any bullying here at this school!"

Then Mrs. Newton said, "Bullies, we hope you got the message. We will take a stand against bullies. All bullies will be dealt with, and there will be consequences for your actions: suspensions, criminal investigations, and even arrests. If there are bullies who need help, we will help you."

She presented a video of students who were bullied, it also included information about bullies who received punishment for their actions. She asked us to stand and repeat after her. "I will not accept bulling from anyone!" Then she closed the meeting.

We left the room chanting, "I will not accept bulling from anyone!"

When we got back to class, I told everyone about the incident. They were quite upset, especially my teacher, Ms. Chapman. She took the time to explain to the class why people should not bully others. She also gave encouraging words to us. "Work hard to achieve, and be proud of yourself. Don't let anyone put you down. Stay positive! Say your prayers, and all will be well. Dare to be different! Believe in yourself!"

After the lecture, Ms. Chapman changed the mood when she announced, "For the last period today, we are going to have a pizza party to celebrate our Spelling Bee Champion." The whole class cheered. We couldn't wait to get our work done and get the party started.

I had an unpleasant experience with bullying. A group of girls waited for me in the hallway. They harassed me and said mean things to me. This girl named Cynthia was a trouble maker. One afternoon as I walked down the hallway, she shouted, "Pinky Winky, you are so stinky." All the other girls in the group with her laughed and started the chant: "Pinky Winky, you are so stinky." Some of the boys heard it, and they joined in.

I was so hurt and upset that I ran all the way to the counselor's office with tears streaming down my face. I knocked loudly on the door. Mrs. Newton opened the door with a concerned look on her face, and she said in a soft kind voice, "Sara, can I help you? What is wrong?" She placed her hand on my shoulder and guided me over to the chair next to her desk. I told her about the incident. I also told her something needed to be done with those bullies. She agreed with me and then she said, "We need to go and talk to the principal."

Mrs. Kelly was very upset to hear about the incident. She sent the counselor to get all the girls who took part in the incident. I looked at their faces as they walked into the principal's office. Some of them looked scared because they knew they were in trouble, but Cynthia came in with her lips pressed together and anger in her eyes.

Before Mrs. Kelly could ask any questions, all of the girls pointed to Cynthia. Then Ellen spoke out. She was not a part of the group, but she'd witnessed what had happened. She said, "I saw Cynthia walk over to the other girls as they were standing there in a group chatting. She said to them, 'Here she comes. When she passes by us, we all will say, Pinky Winky, you are so stinky!'"

Another girl, Eboni said, "She started it, and then she asked us to join in."

Mrs. Kelly replied, "Was that the right thing to do? Why are you listening or following someone who doesn't know how to behave? Would anyone of you in this group like anyone to harass you, to say negative things to you or about you, or to call you a name?"

Cynthia responded, "No one can do that to me. I will punch the person in the mouth."

Mrs. Newton, the counselor, walked over to Cynthia and said, "Girl, you have to learn to behave yourself. Your attitude is bad, and your behavior is bad. You need to stop, think, and change your ways."

Mrs. Kelly got up from her desk and in her loud, authoritative voice said, "All of you did the wrong thing, and you must be disciplined. You will all have lunch-time detention. After lunch, report back to my office." Then she said, "Cynthia, I don't want any bullies in my school. You are a young lady, and you should behave like one. Your punishment for your behavior is two days suspension." Then she turned to Mrs. Newton and said, "Take Cynthia to your office and counsel her. Then call her mother to come in and see me. This school will not accept bullying here."

One would think after these incidences, the students would settle down and behave themselves. But this was not the case, because there were some students who didn't know how to behave.

I thought about this for a long time and wondered why some of them behaved the way they did. Then I came to the conclusion that their home environment influenced their behavior and this also affected the community. Some of them wanted to talk and act like the adults they saw around them.

Part 4

Fights on Dress-Up Day

The big fight that took place confirmed this. The language they used during the fight and the reason why they were fighting proved that children live what they learn.

It was on a Friday, which was a dress-up day. All of the students looked forward to the dress-up days because they loved showing off their outfits, named brand sneakers and designer clothes. However, there was a dress code and specific rules for the girls' attire. Some of the dress-up rules were:

- Do not wear any skinny jeans.

- Do not wear tights without a long blouse.

- Do not wear your back or belly out.

- Absolutely no shorts.

All the girls knew and were drilled on these rules. However, these group of girls decided they were going to wear their tights without long blouses to cover their butts. They were well developed and shapely; their tights highlighted their well-defined shapes. One of the girls told me after the incident that they planned to dress that way to get the attention of the boys. She said, "We are at the age where we have an interest in boys. We wanted them to pay attention to us."

Monica and I -- we always followed the rules. We knew better, and we did better. I wore a pretty pink frilly top with regular jeans and a pink flower in my hair. I also wore a matching pink watch and pink high-top sneakers. Monica wore a blue frilly top similar to mines with jeans and blue high-top sneakers. She also wore a blue headband and blue bubbles on her ponytails. We both knew we looked nice, so we strutted down the hallway as if we were on a Paris Fashion Runway. We were picture perfect.

Shortly after we arrived at school, we saw Pamela and Marilyn coming through the gate. They were dressed like twins, were wearing the same style yellow top with white pants and yellow sandals. They also combed their hair in the same style, with the donut in the back. They knew they looked good, so they were strutting down the hallway. Monica and I ran to meet them. We said, "Hi twins!" Then we all laughed and walked down the hallway together.

That's when we saw the group of girls who enjoyed bothering other students. They were showing off, too. They were loud and obnoxious and ready to make trouble.

These girls were the troublemakers who tried to buck the system. They ignored the rules and did not wear the long top that was required. Each of them wore a top that was a little above the midline.

Allie was wearing hot pink tights with a pink short T-shirt cut off at the waist. If she raised her hand, we could see her stomach. Jackie was wearing red hot tights with a red tank top. She looked sizzling hot. Shanon was wearing highlighter-yellow tights along with a white sleeveless top with a button missing at the bottom of the row. When the wind blew, we could see her stomach. Her color was saying, "You can't miss me. You have to see me." Alma was wearing bright orange tights with a yellow cut-off T-shirt with frills that barely covered her navel. They all stood together in a group.

The mischievous boys saw them and came over to admire them and talk about them. And of course who was leading the pack but Dennis.

Monica, Ellen, Pamela, Marilyn, and I watched them from across the hall. We saw Dennis grab Allie and turn her around so he could look at her shape. The other boys circled the other girls and discussed their shapes. The girls were all giggling and pushing each other. Then, Dennis grabbed each one of them and put them in a line. He turned to the boys and said, "Now tell me who look best?" The boys stood back admiring the girls.

Before they could respond to Dennis's question, Allie stepped out the line, put her hand on her hip, and said, "I look the best. I looked in the mirror this morning and I saw how good I looked when I put my tights on. I can also tell you who don't look so good."

Ellen turned to us and said, "We don't need to look at this nonsense. Let's go to the classroom and review for our math test." We all agreed and went to our classroom. Mrs. Jones was happy to see us, and she said she was pleased with us coming in to review for the test. We sat down and started drilling each other on our multiplication tables from zero to thirteen.

Then Mr. Jones drilled us on tips for word problems. She asked, "If you read a problem that asked for the difference between two numbers; what operation you would use to solve the problem?"

I shouted out, "You have to subtract."

She replied, "You are correct!"

Then Marilyn said, "I know some of the other signal phrases, like 'find the product.'"

Pamela responded, "That means to multiply!"

Mrs. Jones said, "Girls, you are doing well."

Monica said, "I know what to do when it says to find the sum. That means to get the total, and to find the total you have to add."

I had to get my piece in there, so I said, "I know all these operations. I am the best at word problems."

Just then we heard the bell rang. We hurried outside to line up for morning assembly. As we were hustling to line up, we saw and heard a commotion. A large crowd of students was gathered around the spot where we'd left the group of girls in their brightly colored tights with Dennis and the other boys.

Pamela said, "I bet there is a fight going on over there."

Ellen replied, "Maybe the principal is rounding them up for not wearing the appropriate clothing."

Monica said, "Mrs. Kelly should send all of them home—even Dennis."

I responded, "Why Dennis?"

She replied, "Don't you see that the big, baggy jean he's wearing is below his butt? When he bent over earlier to look at the girls, I saw his boxer shorts. That is not right. He is not following the dress code rules for boys."

- No extra big, baggy pants.
- Do not wear pants below the butt.

I had to admit she was right. We walked more briskly, trying to get to the assembly line. At the same time we were curious to find out what was going on. I moved closer to the crowd to see what was happening. That is when I saw the big fight. It was between Allie and Shamon.

I said to one of our classmate who was standing there, "Why are they fighting?"

She proceeded to tell me that Allie started it when she told the boys that she had looked better than the other girls. She was about to say more but the noise from the crowd got our attention. I saw Allie slapped and pushed Shanon. Shanon got angry and she punched Allie in the face. Then the fight was on again. I was nosy so I drew closer to the crowd to see the fight.

Allie started scratching and clawing Shanon like a cat. Shanon jumped back and threw a kick, knocking Allie to the ground. The crowd was cheering them on; half of them were for Allie, and the other half were for Shamon. When Allie landed on the ground, the crowd roared with laughter. Then she managed to scramble up and give Shanon a hard punch in the face. They all heard when the blow landed, and when they looked at Shanon, the area around her eye was swollen. Then they started pulling each other's hair. Shanon bit down on Allie's finger, and Allie let out a yell that brought everyone running, including the principal, to see what was going on. Then the bell rang. It was time for classes to get started.

My classmate and I walked away when we saw the principal. She pushed through the crowd and grab Allie, and Shanon. Mrs. Kelly yelled at them. "Both of you get in my office, now!"

I looked at both girls as they passed by. Their hair was out of place, and they looked so disheveled. I couldn't help but notice Shanon's black eye.

I felt someone pull on my arm, and I turned around. It was Monica. She said, "Those girls just don't know how to behave themselves. They should be suspended."

I responded, "I know Mrs. Kelly will handle it. She already said she will not accept bullying, and the school handbook states the school rules and their consequences. They will definitely be suspended."

We lined up for assembly, and after the morning exercises, Mrs. Kelly instructed everyone to remain there. Her voice was very stern and firm when she addressed the student body. "I will not tolerate any disruptions and disorder in my school. I am here to create a safe learning environment for all of you. Those of you who choose to disrupt the flow of things will be suspended until you learn the rules of this school and learn how to govern yourselves accordingly. How dare those girls disregard the rules with their attire and behavior? They will receive double punishment. And for those of you who think you can get away with it, I am sending a strong message to all. No more dress-up days until I see major changes in behavior. Go back to your classes, and think about this. Teachers, please talk to your classes about their attitudes and behaviors. There are some students who are excellent role models. Get to know them, and follow their examples."

After the assembly, I went into the office to get some worksheets copied and I heard Mrs. Kelly giving Allie and Shanon a good lecture then she called their parents. She said if their behavior didn't change, she did not want them in her school. She also told them she saw them as girls with great potential who could do well if they tried harder. Allie broke down crying and said she would do better. She also apologized for her bad behavior and promised to do better. It took awhile to calm Shanon down because she was upset about her black eye. The principal called Mrs. Cornelius, the nurse, to bring an ice pack. The nurse brought it and instructed Shanon to keep it on her face so that the swelling would go down. Then she looked at Allie's finger. She pointed out the teeth marks where Shamon had bit into it. Mrs. Cornelius told Allie how lucky she was that Shanon did not get a good hold on the finger, because she could have lost it. She also explained to her she had to clean it with alcohol to eliminate the germs. She said if she didn't clean it properly, it could become infected. Mrs. Cornelius poured the alcohol all over the finger and wiped it with some gauze. Then she got some sterile gauze with some antibiotic ointment, wrapped it around the finger, and bandaged it. Throughout the process, Allie was screaming, but Mrs. Cornelius had a firm grip on her. After her finger was well taken care of, Mrs. Cornelius told her to sit in the principal's office.

The principal also called the counselor, Mrs. Newton, to counsel the girls. She came, and they all sat down. Mrs. Newton made them apologize to each other. Then she turned to Allie and said, "The other day when I spoke with your teacher, she told me how creative you were. She also told me you can do your work when you put your mind to it. However, you needed more support from home. I will call your mother to come in and meet with me." Then she turned to Shanon and said, "What happened to you? You were doing so well. What is going on with you?"

Shanon responded, "My mother told me if anybody hit me. I must hit them back. I will not stand there and take it from anyone. This isn't done yet."

Mrs. Kelly said, "What you mean, this isn't done yet? If you think you are going to fight in my school again, you had better think twice about this. If you fight or cause any more disruptions in my school, I will expel you."

Shanon responded, "Did you see what she did to my eye? She'd better not pass my house when she goes to the shop. I am going to deal with her. And I know all the shortcuts she takes to get to school because I take them, too. I will get her back"

Mrs. Newton got up and walked over to Shanon. "You are too pretty to be fighting. A pretty face has to have a pretty mind. I know you think you are tough because you play basketball, but you must remember that manners, respect, and good behavior will help you to succeed in life. Don't try to be a thug. The thug life is not good for you because it can get you killed, or you can end up in jail. Do you want that type of life?" Shanon remained silent. Mrs. Newton continued. "No, you don't. Your gym teacher, Mr. Milligan, told me you are a good basketball player, and if you continue to play well, the possibilities for you are limitless. Who knows, one day I might turn on my television, and there you are, a great basketball star. However, if you continue on the path you are going, you will miss out on those opportunities."

Shanon seemed to be listening. She responded, "You are right. I know I can be a great basketball star. And I want the opportunity to be a professional ballplayer. I know I have to change, and I will work on it. I have a bad temper and can fly off the handle quickly." Shanon realized her hopes, dreams, and goals for herself would help her to change her attitude. "I am sorry for hitting you, Allie. It's over. I am not mad anymore. We can still be friends. No more hard feelings."

Mrs. Kelly and Mrs. Newton were happy they got through to Shanon. They acknowledged that she came from a rough neighborhood, and her home life was also rough. Mrs. Kelly decided she would mentor her and nurture her.

Then Mrs. Kelly called their parents and informed them they had to come to the school for a disciplinary hearing in regard to their children's behavior. Allie started to cry again. When Mrs. Kelly asked her why she was crying; she said, "I don't want my mom to come to the school and embarrass me. If she is drunk, she will come here and curse all kinds of dirty words at me, and then she will jump on me and give me some blows. Please don't call her. I will start following the rules."

Mrs. Kelly responded, "That is good to know." Then she spoke to the girls about their attire. She told them they did not follow the dress code, and she asked them why.

Shanon said, "Cynthia told them to dress this way so that we can get the boys' attention."

Mrs. Newton responded, "Your focus should not be on boys but on your school work. There will be time enough for boys, but right now you need to get your priorities straight. Put your education first."

Mrs. Kelly added, "I will be monitoring all of the fifth and sixth grade girls more closely. We have to make sure they keep their focus." Then she told Mrs. Newton, "You need to have more interactive counseling sessions with the fifth and six graders. Find out from them what their future plans are and what goals they have set for themselves." Mrs. Kelly told the girls to wait outside until their parents arrived.

I wanted to hear their conversation, so I followed closely behind them as they stepped out the office. We were facing down the hallway and we saw Cynthia trotting through the gate. Cynthia was all out of breath. We also noticed that the white top she was wearing with her green tights was short. It was above her waist, and her navel was showing. She was very curvy, and everything printed out in the tights and was prominently visible. They turned and looked at each other with their mouths opened wide. Then Allie said, "We can't let her walk in to a suspension. Let's update her on the happenings, and we will also tell her what Mrs. Kelly said about breaking the dress code rules." They ran to meet her, pulled her aside, and quickly gave her an update.

I heard Cynthia said she was late for school, and she was on her way to the office to get a late pass. She told them this was not a good day for her. She woke up late, she didn't have time to get breakfast, and she couldn't find the blouse she wanted to wear. She said she searched everywhere, but she couldn't find her green top to wear with her green tights. Then she said it didn't matter anyway, because it would have shown more of her skin. It had splits on both sides, it was short, and it tied up in the front.

Cynthia told them she didn't want to get suspended, so she would go back home. She told them her mom went to work, so no one would know she didn't go to school. She loved being home by herself because she could talk to boys on the phone. She pushed pass them and ran back through the gate. Shanon shouted for her to come back, but she ran even faster. I quickly walked away as I saw Shanon and Allie walking back to the front of the office to wait for their parents.

Later, I was told by one of my classmates that she
and some other students passed by and saw the girls
sitting outside the office. They were curious about
what the girls did. Some knew and had smirks on
their faces, as if they were glad the troublemakers got
caught. She said Allie gave them a mean look and
threaten to go after them and shout in their faces,
"Mind your own business!" Shanon reminded her of
the promises they'd made to themselves, Mrs. Kelly,
and Mrs. Newton. Shanon stayed in her seat and
hung her head because she didn't want anyone to see
her black eye.

I went back to the office to get some pencils, and
as some students passed by, I saw Allie put her hand
behind her back. I guess she didn't want any of the
students passing by to see her finger bandaged up. I
felt sorry for them. They looked like two wounded

soldiers out of battle. Both of them must be secretly feeling pain and they seemed anxious to get the rest of this situation over with. I wondered, *what was taking their moms so long to come?*

Then Shanon said, "This was the longest time they had to wait at the office." Suddenly we heard Shamon's mother's voice. "I had to leave my job and come here for nonsense. Somebody is going to get it today. I don't have time for this. I am losing money and can't afford it. Let me see who this girl is who fought with my daughter. I hope my daughter whooped her good. I told you not to let anyone hit you and get away with it!" She was walking down the hallway, talking loudly, and motioning for Shanon to come to her.

Just then Allie heard her mom voice shouting out her name. "Allie, where are you? Girl, come here. Didn't I tell you to go to school and learn your lesson?

Why are you following bad company and doing the wrong things?"

Before Allie could respond to her mom's question, Shanon's mom lunged at Allie and tried to grab her. She said, "Don't you ever put your hand on my child!"

As she reached for Allie, Allie's mom pushed Shanon mother away and said, "Now, don't you put your hand on my child!"

Then Shanon mother threw down her purse, jumped in front of Allie's mom, and slapped her. Allie's mom grabbed the woman's spaghetti strap blouse and ripped it off of her.

I screamed out, "Mrs. Kelly come out here! Parents are fighing."

Everyone in the office heard the commotion and came out to see what was going on. Then I heard Mrs. Kelly shout, "Call the police! This can't happen in my school. What example are both of you setting for the children? This is embarrassing and shameful. These adults are behaving worse than the children. No parent should come on this campus to disrupt my students' education!"

An audience of teachers, students, and custodians gathered around the event. They were laughing, clapping, and pointing as the two parents latched on to each other, pulling and tugging at each other's hair and clothes. This seemed to be great entertainment for everyone, especially Allie and Shanon.

Mrs. Kelly ordered everyone to return to class or get back to their duties. Then she turned her attention to the parents. "Stop this right now!" Her loud voice shocked them back to reality when she shouted, "Call the police! Call 911"

Someone in the office shouted back, "The police is on the way."

The fighting stopped and both ladies took their daughters and went through the gate. Everyone shook their heads in disbelief. Mrs. Newton turned to the students and said, "Students, you see what can happen when you don't follow rules."

The police came, but the parents had already left. They took statements from the principal, the counselor, and some others who had witnessed the fight. Some of the students who didn't have their facts straight wanted to talk to the police. The police made it clear to them they only needed the facts and not their opinion.

Some of the other students stayed clear - especially the younger ones. They were afraid of the police. One of the teachers asked them why they were scared of the police. One of the boys was bold enough to say, "When I don't behave, my mom says she will call the police for me, and they will take me to jail. I don't want to go to jail, and I don't want to see the police." The teacher and his classmates laughed.

For the rest of the day, the talks and discussions were about the fights. This was a day to remember. Some of the students said it should be called fight day instead of dress-up day. The other three girls who did not wear the correct clothes thought they got away with it, but Mrs. Kelly sent for them, too. "Come to the office," she told them. "You are suspended for three days for not following the dress code. Your ringleaders and your friends will receive the same three days, plus four days for fighting." They were shocked to learn their fate. This was not their lucky day.

Part 5

Dennis's Meeting with the Principal

On my way to the office I saw Dennis walking to the office. He looked worried. I usually go to the office after school to do some volunteer work, and I was sorting some papers when he walked in. I glanced at him from the side because I didn't want him to see me watching him. He might have given me the evil eye, or he might even be thinking I reported his baggy pants below his butt, but I had not. However, I was in the office when Mrs. Kelly sent the secretary to get the girls, then she gave me a note to give to his teacher. I guess the note was for him to come to the office. He too probably thought he had gotten away with the attire and with his contribution to the fight, but he should have known better. There was always someone around to report him.

Mrs. Kelly saw him coming, and she said, "Dennis, you had better pull your pants up before you come into my office."

When Dennis heard Mrs. Kelly in that tone of voice, he knew he had to get his act together. He swiftly pulled up his pants, looked down and make sure his shoelaces were tied, and then quickly took his comb out of his pocket and passed it through his hair. He walked into the principal's office with his head down, as if to show guilt and remorse. Mrs. Kelly was not fooled by that because she knew Dennis well.

Dennis said, "Good afternoon, Mrs. Kelly!" in a low, monotone voice.

Mrs. Kelly replied, "Good afternoon, Dennis," in a vexed tone. Then she said, "Why did you wear those pants today? You know the dress code says no baggy or sagging pants. No pants below the butt. Yet you choose to wear them today. Do you know the origin of these pants below the butt look? Did you know this look came from prisoners who had no belt to keep their pants up? Their belts were taken from them; just in case they were suicidal, they couldn't hang themselves. There is also another side to the look. Some prisoners in jail used it to send a sign to other prisoners. Is this a sign you want to send around here?"

The look on Dennis's face said it all. His facial expression showed that he was upset, stunned, and puzzled. He paused for a moment and then said, "No, Mrs. Kelly, I am not sending any sign. I thought it was a style. I see lots of other boys doing it. I thought it was a cool thing to do."

Mrs. Kelly responded, "Now that you have heard the truth about the style - are you still going to wear your pants like that?"

Dennis replied, "I am thinking about it, but I don't think I will."

Even though they were in the inner office, I heard everything. Dennis didn't close the door when he walked in, and Mrs. Kelly didn't close it, either. Maybe she wanted me to hear what was happening, or she was too preoccupied to close it. Maybe it was my curiosity or my concern, So I sat in a chair that gave me a good view into the principal's office, and I was mesmerized as I took it all in.

I heard Mrs. Kelly ask Dennis, "Do you want to challenge or test me? You are not a man. You are a little boy. Conduct yourself accordingly. You are trying to be a bully and a tough guy, but underneath all of that, you are a sweet, smart, handsome, and intelligent young man. Take off the mask. Let the real you be seen."

When I heard her saying those words about him, I secretly agreed with her. I thought some of the same things, too.

She continued to lecture him. "You will be suspended for three days for breaking the school rules. You have chosen to go down the wrong path. You are making bad decisions that will get you into trouble. Do you want to be a gangster?"

I saw Dennis screwed up his face as he stood there starring.

I wondered why he was not responding to Mrs. Kelly. She kept repeating her question as she got louder and louder.

Later, he told me his thoughts. He said, I thought, *who does she think she is, talking to me like that? I wear what I want. This is a brand-new pair of pants I got for dress-up day. And what is she talking about gangsters? My buddies and I are cool. We just want to show our classmates that we run things. We are the big men on campus, and they must respect us and fall in line. I don't like people shouting at me or telling me what to do. This is a dumb school. I can't wait to get out of here. I know when I go to junior high, I will run things. I know my buddies have my back. We are tough, and no one will mess with us. This woman needs to hurry up talking so I can get out of here.*

Then he said he heard the principal's loud voice and this interrupted his thoughts. "Dennis, are you listening to me? Are you hearing what I am saying to you?"

"But Mrs. Kelly, I didn't do anything wrong."

Mrs. Kelly replied, "Boy, you have done a lot wrong. Do you need me to remind you? The other day you acted like a real jerk when you hit Sara with that rock in her back. Stop that abusive behavior. You will end up in jail and wear your pants the way you want to wear it. Is this what you want?"

Dennis hung his head in shame. Then he said, "No, Mrs. Kelly, I will make a change."

Mrs. Kelly said, "Dennis, come closer to me, and let me give you a bit of advice. Drop this gangster attitude. You don't have to behave that way to make friends or to get people to like you. Change your behavior, and you will see how many people love you. We all do. We love you, but we don't like the things you do. If you promise to make the change, I will let you in on a little secret I found out about you the other day. It is an interesting secret, and I am sure you would like to know what it is. Would you like to know what it is?" Dennis looked at Mrs. Kelly, and she had this big grin on her face. He said that he thought, this must be something good, and he wondered what it was. He thought, *Should I make this promise? What if I can't keep it? What would my buddies think of me if they saw a change in my behavior? They might think I am too soft and find other friends. My buddy Keith might become the leader of the group. He backs me up, or he copies the things I do. No, I don't think I will make any promises.* He also said he was anxious to know what the interesting secret was.

Then I saw Mrs. Kelly hold Dennis by the wrist and pull him closer to her desk. She looked him straight in the eyes and said, "Dennis, don't miss out on the opportunity I am giving you. Do you want to make the change? Do you want to hear the secret? Tell me now what you want to do. It is all up to you. Do you need some more time to think about this? Sit down in that chair; I will give you five minutes more. After the five minutes are up, this special offer is no longer on the table. I am telling you that if you miss this one, you might never get another one."

Dennis sat in the chair, folded his arms and put his hand under his chin. He looked as if he was deep in thought. And he sure was. He said he thought about the way Mrs. Kelly acted and spoke to him. He wondered, did she really care about him? Then he said to himself, *she must care. Otherwise she would not have taken the time out of her busy schedule to counsel me. She could have just given me my punishment and let me go. But she took the time to talk to me.* This made him feel good to know the principal cared about him. He told himself, *now I have to change my behavior so that my teacher can care about me, too.*

He looked up at the clock on the wall. To him, the short hand seemed to be going around very quickly. Soon his five minutes would be up, and he hadn't made his decision yet. Then he said to himself, *I will make it now, but it is only because I want to know the secret.*

I saw Mrs. Kelly working through the mounds of paperwork on her desk. I knew she had deadlines to meet, documents that required her signature, teacher's lesson plans to review, and correspondence to catch up on. However, I saw her keeping a keen eye on

Dennis. I knew she was hoping and praying that she got through to him. Later, she told how she heard him whispered her name, but she kept right on working.

I observed her moving around the papers on her desk. I wondered what next.

Dennis repeated himself, but he said it a little louder this time. "Mrs. Kelly."

She replied, "Yes, Dennis? Have you made your decision?"

"Yes, Mrs. Kelly, I have. Now, what is the secret?"

Mrs. Kelly put down the papers she was working on so that she could give him her full attention. Then she said, "You will have to state clearly what your decision is. We both have to have a definite understanding and agreement."

I wanted to hear what he was saying, so I picked up the message the secretary, Mrs. Warner, had given me just a minute ago to give to the principal. I was glad for the opportunity to go to the inner office. I knocked on the door, excused myself, and handed Mrs. Kelly the note.

As I slowly walked back through the door, I heard Dennis respond. "I promise to change my behavior, follow the school rules, and become a more positive influence for my friends."

Mrs. Kelly was so surprised. She got up from her desk and hugged him. Then she said, "Wow! Young man, you impressed me. I am now happy to tell you my secret. I was told you have a secret admirer. I can't and won't tell you who it is. You will have to find out for yourself. But I can tell you one thing: if your behavior doesn't change, you will never know who it is."

Dennis told me later he had to admit the encounter in the office was more than he could take. The principal hugged him. After he had been in her office so many times for his bad behavior, still she told him something he didn't know. He liked what she told him, and after she said it, he had such a big grin on his face. He felt his heart racing with excitement. He decided he was going on a mission to find out who was this person. He couldn't wait to get out of the office to start his detective work. He thought about calling his buddies to help him out. However, he changed his mind and decided to keep the secret to himself.

He also said after Mrs. Kelly dismissed him, he walked out of the office with his head held high. This was a change compared to the other times when he came out of the office with his head hanging low. He even forgot about the punishment he had received for not following the rules about the dress code.

As I watched him walk out, I felt happy for him. He looked different. In fact, I must admit he looked even more handsome. I couldn't help but wonder who this secret admirer was. I wondered how and when he was going to find out.

Part 6

Sharing Stories with Monica/
Conversations with Dennis

I couldn't wait to tell Monica all that I'd seen and heard. This was a lot for us to talk about. I had to swear her to secrecy. I shouldn't talk about this, but I had to share this with my best friend. We had lots to talk about: all the events of the day; the girls' attire, the fight, their parents' fight, and Dennis's promise. I decided to ask Mom and Dad if I could spend the night at Monica's house. We could do our homework, eat dinner, bathe, and then we go to her room and talk. We would skip watching television, as we usually did. We had more drama to talk about than what was on television.

I quickly finished sorting my last batch of papers, and then I tidied up my work area. I said good-bye to Mrs. Warner and Mrs. Kelly and hurried out of the office. I ran to the library to tell Monica I was spending the night with her. She was so shocked and surprised, and she asked, "What's going on, Sara? It is not the weekend yet."

We both laughed, and then I gave her a quick and brief explanation. Before we ran to the gate, we stopped in the office and asked Mrs. Warner for permission to call Monica's mom. Monica asked her if I can sleepover. Then I heard Monica say, "Thanks Mom!" and hung up the phone. Then she turned to me and said, "Mom says, it's all right for you to sleep over." I was happy to know our plans were going well. Then I said, "Monica, let's go to the gate to wait for my parents. We ran to the school gate to meet Mom and Dad. Shortly after we were at the gate they pulled up and we got in the car. I asked them if I could spend the night at Monica's house. They both responded with a yes. They didn't question me because they knew that when Monica and I had a test coming up we usually spend the night at each other's house and study together. I also told them that Monica was coming for the ride with me to pick up my overnight bag.

Dad asked, "Does Monica's mom know you are spending the night?"

We said, "Yes, we called her from the office phone."

Mom replied, "You both seem to have things worked out. You are responsible girls with good heads on your shoulders. I am pleased that both of you are best friends. I want you to look out for each other at all times. Don't let anyone or anything break your friendship."

We got my things and went back to Monica's house. We followed the plan - did our homework, ate dinner, bathed, and went to Monica's room. We talked about the day's events, and we laughed about the fights. Then we talked about Dennis. Monica said she felt bad that he got suspended because she didn't think he was a bad boy. She also hinted to me that she thought she liked him. I was surprised to hear her say that. Many times she was upset with him for the things he did, especially that time when he hit me with the rock. We talked so much that we didn't realize it was so late, until Monica's mom stuck her head in the door and told us to turn off the lights and go to sleep. Our last words to each other before we fell off to sleep were, "I hope Dennis changes his attitude and behavior."

I was surprise the next day when Dennis decided to have a conversation with me. He told me the visit to the principal's office was an important one. He also said he learned so much and gained a lot including the love and respect of the principal. As he spoke, I felt that Dennis knew down in his heart that all of this was really worth the change. He went home and thought long and hard about this. I don't think he wanted to continue down the path that he was going. He said didn't want to end up in jail with his pants sagging below his butt and he didn't want to send the wrong message to anyone. The he reassured me that his decision was final to make the change in his behavior. Dennis kept smiling when he talked about what Mrs. Kelly had told him about a secret admirer.

He kept saying, "I wondered who could it be, I hope it was not one of those noisy, rowdy, troublesome girls. He also said, *I don't want any of those girls. My girl has to be intelligent and beautiful. I hope I won't be disappointed when I find out.*

I laugh even now when I recall what he said.

Part 7

Recalling Events Leading up to my Promotion Exercise

There are so many memories of my elementary school days. The most memorable one is my sixth grade Promotional Exercise.

I recalled Monica was the one who suggested we form a promotion committee to give input on some of the decisions that would be made for the promotional exercise. We presented the idea to our class and the other sixth grade class, and they agreed.

We discussed the attire. During the discussions the boys shouted out, "We will let Monica pick the color! We already know if we let Sara pick, she will pick pink." Everyone laughed.

I walked over to her and whispered in her ear. "You can choose the style, but please let me pick the color." She nodded her head in agreement.

Some of the girls agreed with the boys that Monica should choose the attire. Monica responded, "I will go to the fabric store and pick a pattern. Some of you girls can go with me and help me pick the pattern." Paulette, Shermena, and Feelena said they would go with Monica to select the pattern.

Then Hyacinth said, "So Sara, tell us what you had in mind."

I replied, "I have been dreaming about this from since the school year began. I envisioned all the girls in a beautiful pastel pink ballroom gown, and the boys in their pastel pink shirt with black pants and a black tie."

Dennis, who was the most outspoken of the boys and whom I considered the troublemaker, shouted out, "Really? No way! I will not wear a pink shirt. Pink is for girls." Everyone laughed.

I turned to Monica and wittingly said, "What style do you think the dress should be?"

Monica replied, "I was thinking of a knee-length dress with ruffles around the neck and the hemline."

Shirley spoke up. "Yes, I can see myself in that style. I like dresses with ruffles."

Joyce said, "Yes, a pink dress with ruffles will look dashing and smashing."

The other girls agreed. I had to think quickly about getting Dennis and the other boys to agree on the pink shirt. I said, "Boys, if you agree to wear the pink shirt, I will ask the principal if we can have a dance party a couple days before the promotion exercise.

I will use my most convincing speech to get her to agree."

There was a pause from all the whisperings, and then Dennis stood up and said, "Well, that sounds like a good idea. Boys, what do you think?"

The boys said, "We can agree to that, but only if we can have a dance party, and if all the girls agree to wear blue outfits to the party."

I replied, "We have to get permission from the principal." Then I assured them I would do my best to get her approval. I had to keep my promise to the boys. I wanted us all to get along, and this was also a good way to get Dennis to change his behavior and stop being a bully.

After the meeting I went to the principal's office and greeted the secretary. "Good morning, Mrs.

Warner. May I speak to the principal, please? I will just be a few minutes."

Mrs. Warner was a very warm, charming, and caring person. We could approach her anytime, and if we had a problem, she would help us solve it. She was the right person to sit at that front desk. I would be in the office on various occasions and hear her answer the phone. She was real professional in her tone, and she spoke clearly and with correct grammar.

She stopped what she was doing and looked at me with such a warm, reassuring smile. "Yes, Sara, you may speak to her. I will let her know you are here." She got up from her desk and walked into the inner office.

I took the time to get my thoughts together. I would start by telling Mrs. Kelly how much I respected her as my principal, and about how most of us students appreciated the innovative, energetic, fun, and firm way she ran the school. I also would thank her for the way she handled my bullying situation. Then I would tell her why I was there.

As I was going over these thoughts in my head, Mrs. Warner came out and told me, "You can go in now."

I walked in straight and tall with held my head held high. I felt very confident because I had to represent my classmates well. I said, "Good morning, Mrs. Kelly!"

She responded with a bright and cheerful, "Good morning, Sara! Please have a seat."

I sat upright in the seat and did not slouch. I had charm, poise, and beauty, and I knew it, so I showed it. Then I began with my compliments and then my thank-you. I was now ready to state the purpose of my visit. I explained to Mrs. Kelly the reason why

I was requesting permission for the dance party. I also explained the benefits to us students to have it, such as social interaction, boosting our morale for a celebration of moving on to seventh grade, but most important to show Dennis we could all get along and have fun.

She listened intently and nodded firmly in agreement. She thanked me for coming forward with the idea, and she promised to assign a committee to help us with it. I left her office skipping and jumping. I couldn't wait to find Monica and tell her the good news.

I caught up with Monica later that day. I told her Mrs. Kelly granted us permission for the dance party and she also said that she would get a committee to help us. Monica was happy with the news. She also told me that over the weekend she, her mom, and the other girls went to the fabric store and picked out the pattern for the dress. I thanked her for her input and support, and then I told her I would like for her and her mom to join me and my mom to select the material on Friday afternoon after school. Then I said, "Monica, we have to meet with the other girls to tell them about the little trick we have up our sleeve for the dance party."

We met with the girls after school and told them what the plan was. I said, "We will all come to the party in our blue outfits, but halfway through it, we will change to our pink ones and surprise the boys." As usual, girls loved to impress boys and get their attention. They were all on board about making the switch. We swore them to secrecy, and I told them, "Remember, our lips are sealed!" They laughed, and we left the meeting in good spirits. Erica and Eboni thanked me for the idea of surprising the boys; they said they couldn't wait to see the expressions on the boy's faces.

The next day our teacher Mrs. Jones told us the principal had spoken to her. Mrs. Jones was heading up the committee. She also said there would be a meeting on Thursday afternoon, and parents and students were invited.

Monica and I loved the idea that we were going to be a part of the planning and organizing of the dance party. For the rest of the week the talk among the students was all about the event. The meeting went well. We agreed on the decorations: rainbow streamers in pastel colors, balloons in pastel colors, and tinsel colors of red, blue, and silver to highlight and enhance the other decorations.

As we gathered together and looked through the catalog, we got excited and carried away. We told the committee what we wanted and how we wanted it. Then we discussed the ideas and agreed on some of it. We also agreed to highlight the best dressed boy and girl. We ordered the flute glasses, noisemakers, and confetti. The boys wanted top hats, and the girls wanted little princess tiaras. We were planning to have a ball.

The last few weeks leading up to promotion was very hectic. We held several fundraisers for our promotion luncheon. There were cake sales, and everyone always knew which cakes I donated, whether it was a whole one or cupcakes. My color and style were my trademark - pink icing with a pink flower design. My mom also donated pink sugar cakes. They were the top seller at the fundraiser. Everyone wanted a pink sugar cake. We never had enough of them. The boys' group decided to have a lemonade stand as their fundraiser contribution. Our class planned to buy our teachers flowers because we wanted to show them how much we appreciated them. I reminded my classmates of the hard work our teachers had done to get us to this point. I also had some influence with the boys and their lemonade stand. They sold pink lemonade, of course!

Our sixth grade class worked hard. We all wanted to move ahead as a class, and so we organized a tutorial group to help those who were falling behind. We studied together in small groups. We drilled those who were behind, especially in spelling, because this was one of my best subjects. For those who had difficulty reading, we had them read aloud to us. We reviewed our social studies and science notes, and we also did math practice exercises.

Whenever our teacher, Mrs. Jones, announced a test was coming up, we would stay after school and prepare for it. We were determined to do our best. Behaviors improved, test scores increased, and everyone was motivated. Our teacher commended us on the great job we did. "This sixth grade class will be well prepared for seventh grade, and it is also the most competitive and motivated class." We felt good about ourselves to hear our teacher saying positive thing about us. We were motivated to do our best.

The dance party turned out to be a blast. We walked into the auditorium, which was transformed into a beautiful room. The DJ was playing the dance hall music we requested. The boys came in looking all dapper and GQ. They looked like gentleman of quality, and the girls looked stunning in their blue outfits. We huddled together to reassure each other that we were still going to put the plan in motion. We high-fived each other and seal the deal.

Everyone finally trickled in, and the dance was on. We even did the Electric Slide - the faster version, to a calypso beat. The boys were really kicking it, trying to impress the girls. We all got cold drinks to cool us off. We moved around the room, sipped our drinks, and chatted with each other.

After awhile I noticed the boys went over to one corner of the room. They appeared to be in a serious discussion. I tried to get closer to eavesdrop on their conversation, but Monica stopped me and told me it was time for us to change. I gathered the rest of the girls, and we went to the bathroom to change. We had arranged with the DJ to play the song "Girls Just Want to Have Fun" when we came out in our pink. After we were dressed, we sent the word out to start playing our song. Some of us came out singing and stepping; the others came out prancing and dancing, but we were all shouting, "Girls just want to have fun!"

What a surprise we had when the lights were turned on, and there were the boys nicely dressed in their pink shirts, waving at as and singing, "Boys just want to have fun!! We stopped dead in our tracks. They walked over to us, and Dennis was leading the pack. He was also wearing his top hat, and he had a cane in his left arm and he was swinging it around. Each boy hooked on to a girl's arm. There were not enough boys, so some of the boys ended up with two girls. We danced around in a circle until the song was finished.

Then I said, "How did this happen?

Dennis walked over to me and said, "Do you think you girls are the only one who can think smart? Boys can also think! We are smart, and we did it in pink, so what do you think?"

I burst out laughing and then gave him a quick hug. His face looked so cute and handsome, and he broke out into a smile that lit up his face. I called Monica and told her how the boys planned the same thing we did, and it was Dennis's idea. She was surprised and impressed at the change she had seen in Dennis's mood and behavior.

We enjoyed the rest of the party, with lots of food and drinks. Then it was time to announce who were the best dressed boy and girl. The judging team was made up of the committee members; they walked around throughout the event, making their notes.

Mrs. Kelly said it was time to announce the winners. Everyone gather around, and the excitement was building. I heard Lelia say, "It had better be me. I know I look good, and all the boys love me." Monica nudged me in the side, and we snickered to ourselves.

Then Cheryl said, "I wish it could be me." I kept quiet, secretly wishing it would be me.

Mrs. Kelly said, "And the best dressed boy is … Dennis Benders!" There was loud applause, whistles from the other boys, and shouting from the girls. I found myself clapping as loudly as I could. Dennis stepped out proudly with a big grin from ear to ear. A sash was pinned on him that said "Best Dressed Boy." Then he received all his other gifts, but he told me later the best gift he received was the hug from me.

All the girls ran up to him, pushing and shoving to give him a hug. This was unbelievable. In the past he was one of the bullies with a bad attitude who liked to fight and make trouble. Now he had changed. He was well liked and was fun to be around.

The next announcement was the name of the best-dressed girl. All the girls huddled together, and some of them held hands nervously. Ellen came over quickly and whispered in my ear, "I know who it is."

Before she could say who she thought it was, Mrs. Kelly said, "Let's have a drum roll!" The DJ obliged, and then she said, "The best-dressed girl is none other than … Sara Primus!"

I heard my name, but for a moment I couldn't move. The screams and shouts deafened me. Then I felt Monica's hand on my arm guiding me forward to receive my sash: "Best Dressed Girl."

The boys made a big circle around me, stomping and clapping. Then the girls joined the circle. I wiped a tear of joy from my eye. As I lifted my head up, I saw Dennis leaving the circle and walking toward me. I got a bit nervous and wondered what he was up to now. Dennis simply took my hand and twirled me around. I felt like a princess. Then he said, "May I have this dance?"

I responded, "Yes, you may!" Everyone said we looked so cute dancing together. I enjoyed the dance.

The fun of the dance was over. The next few was focused on the final exams. We got back into our groups and put extra effort into studying. We had the exam schedule, and we planned our strategy for each one.

The first day of the exams, everyone was nervous—even me. Mrs. Jones said that we would do the challenging subjects first. The first day was math, and there were word problems, equations, geometry, and fractions. We were prepared for this. We had done lots of practice problems. I hoped everyone passed this test. I looked around the room, and everyone was on task. I saw scratch paper being used up, and I saw satisfied looks on faces as they worked out the answers. This was encouraging. We all kept working steadily, and no one asked for bathroom or water breaks.

Then I heard Mrs. Jones announce, "Only fifteen more minutes to complete the test. All of you have been working for the past one hour and forty-five minutes. I know all of you are doing your best. As I walk around, I looked at some of your work and answers, and I am pleased with what I saw."

Shortly after her announcement, various students from around the room put down their pencils and raised their hands to indicate they were finished.

The pattern continued throughout the week for the other subjects: reading, language arts, social studies, and science. After each exam, during our breaks or lunch time, we got together and discussed how we did. The discussions were encouraging. We all felt that we did well.

Mrs. Jones confirmed this when she gave us back our graded exams. She said, "Some of you did extremely well, and some of you did good, but I am pleased to announce that all of you have passed on to the seventh grade!" The classroom went into an uproar. The boys drummed on the desks, the girls screamed, and everyone stood on their chairs. Mrs. Jones had to blow her whistle to get the class back in order.

Part 8

Promotion Day

Promotion day came we were all excited. In a few minutes we should all be lined up and marching unto the stage. I could hardly contain myself. I looked forward for this moment for a long time. We were going back and forth to pose for pictures. We looked gorgeous in our pink ruffle dresses and accessories. I looked in the mirror several times before I left the house, and I was pleased with the way I looked. Several appearances in the mirror and all the other excitement made me forgot to pick up my folder with my speech.

My mom and dad were busy trying to get me out of the house. Mom said, "We have to be early because I want a front-row seat. I have to see and hear my daughter give her speech. She is the top student in her class and she is so smart!"

Dad added, "That's my Pinky! She has my genes, and that is why she is so smart."

Mom responded. "Just remember that half of those genes are mines. You only have fifty percent." They both laughed.

I was making my last trip to the mirror when I heard their conversation, and I smiled. Then Dad shouted out, "It is time to go!" That was when I rushed out of the house and forgot to pick up my speech.

Only when Mrs. Kelly announced it was time to line up, I realized I didn't have my speech. I ran into the auditorium to find Mom and Dad and told them that I had forgotten my speech. Dad raced out of there so quickly that I couldn't believe it—in a flash he was gone. Mom tried her best to keep me calm. I was so upset with myself that I wanted to cry, but I didn't. I told myself, *you are too pretty to cry. Not now, not here!* I regained my composure and walked back outside to join the lineup. I knew my dad would be back soon.

I walked over to Monica, who stood there clutching her speech tightly in her hand and I told her what happened. She started biting her nails on the other hand; she always did this when she was nervous. I reassured her everything would be all right. She was the second highest honor student, and I was the first. We both would be delivering our speeches.

Mrs. Jones started lining us up in alphabetical order. My last name was Primus, so I was near the back of the line. I looked around nervously for my father, and then I heard the music start. The line moved forward slowly. My heart and my thoughts started racing. *What if Dad doesn't make it back in time? Did he find the folder with the speech on the table?* Then I said to myself, *you are smart enough to think on your feet. Relax yourself and get your thoughts together.* After I said this, I started breathing easier.

Then I heard a familiar voice; it was my dad. "I have it, Sara. Stop worrying." He handed me the folder and then he gave me a hug. That was the best thing that ever happened to me.

We marched into the auditorium and took our places. The promotion exercise program began. It was short, so Monica and I were soon called to do our speeches.

I addressed the invited and honored guests, and then I thanked my principal and teacher. I addressed the sixth grade classes, particularly my classmates. I l told them how proud I was of them, and I recalled all the things we had accomplished together. I ended my speech with an invitation for all the boys to stand, and then I asked the parents, "How do you think these boys look?" I heard some of the responses: smart, handsome, good, and sharp! Then the parents applauded them. I did the same with the girls, and the parents responded: beautiful, intelligent, and gorgeous. The shouts and applause were unending.

Then I asked all the sixth graders to tell their parents why they looked so awesome, and in unison they replied, "We look smart in pink, and we can think!"

Respond to Sara's Story

Make a list of new words you found in the story.

Find the meaning of the words you listed.

Which part of the story did you connect with?

What was the most interesting part of the story?

Can you list some teachable moments in the story?

More..About the Author

Patricia Maynard has been a professional educator for more than twenty-five years. She is very passionate about teaching and learning. She believes that all children can learn. She has taught all the primary grades, from Kindergarten to Sixth.

She was recognized as an outstanding teacher in the St. Thomas/ St. John School District. She was also honored for her contributions to educating the children of the Virgin Islands. She has made presentations at various Professional Workshops and Organizations, such as the American Federation of Teachers Mini Quest and Lockhart Elementary School Professional

Day, and a Motivational Presentation to the Wesley Methodist Cotillion Contestant.

Her educational background includes a Bachelor of Arts in Elementary Education, a Master of Arts in School Administration, Master's in Public Administration and a Curriculum Specialist Degree. She is certified as a highly qualified teacher and also has certification as an Assistant Principal.

She is very active in her church and community. She is also the founder of the Progressive and Ambitious Girls Club and the Know It and Grow It Boys Gardening Club.

She was the coordinator of various activities:

Spelling Bee

Communication Arts Showcase

Marcelli Cheerleading groups

Miss Marcelli Pageant Show

She is a Sunday school teacher; a member of the Wesleyan Academy School Board; and a member of the St. Thomas and St. John Library Association.

Presently she is an assistant principal at Joseph Gomez Elementary School.

In spite of her hectic schedule, she is committed to her family. She is married to Paul Maynard, M D. She has three sons, Paul Jr. and a set of identical twins, Dwight and Dwayne.

She is an avid reader and enjoys writing. When she can find the time, she enjoys going to the beach.

Printed in the United States
By Bookmasters